PARKER 2014

For Eleni and Gabrielle

First American Edition 2014
Kane Miller, A Division of EDC Publishing

Text and illustrations copyright © 2014 Peter Carnavas
First published in Australia by New Frontier Publishing
Translation rights arranged through Australian Licensing Corporation

For information contact:
Kane Miller, A Division of EDC Publishing
P.O. Box 470663
Tulsa, OK 74147-0663

www.kanemiller.com
www.edcpub.com
www.usbornebooksandmore.com

Library of Congress Control Number: 2013939902
Printed and bound in China
1 2 3 4 5 6 7 8 9 10
ISBN: 978-1-61067-245-0

THE BOY
ON THE
PAGE

PETER CARNAVAS

Kane Miller
A DIVISION OF EDC PUBLISHING

One quiet morning, a small boy landed on the page.

At first, there was nothing else.

Then very slowly, a world began to appear.

New life emerged. Things started to grow...
and so did the boy.

But as he wandered through his new world,

one question troubled him.

Why was he here?

The boy looked around the page then before he knew it,

he was doing all sorts of things.
He rolled down a hill.

He rode a horse.

He caught a shiny, silver fish.

He planted a tree.

He paddled a canoe.

He played an accordion.

He saved a small animal.

He stood in the pouring rain.

He painted a portrait.

The boy grew up and he fell in love.

He climbed a mountain.

He saw the whole world in somebody's eyes.

He built a house.

He gave someone lunch...

and a place to stay.

He grew vegetables.

He trained a dog.

He put out a fire.

But every now and then, as the moon rolled through the deep blue sky, he still wondered why he had landed on the page.

Looking for answers, he tried something he had
never tried before.

Jumping off the page ...

... only to tumble straight back.

And waiting for him there
was every thing he had ever made,
every animal he had ever cared for
and every person he had ever loved.

At last, he knew.
He knew why he was here.